D0897267

FREEDOM
FLIGHT

SUPPORT
AND
DEFEND

FREEDOM
FLIGHT

PATRICK JONES

darbycreek
MINNEAPOLIS

The author wishes to thank Susan Olson, Professional Counselor, M.Ed., LPC, for her expertise on military families and thoughtful review of manuscripts in the Support and Defend series, and Judith Klein for her proofreading and copyediting wizardry.

Copyright © 2015 by Patrick Jones

All rights reserved. International copyright secured. No part of this book may be reproduced, stored in a retrieval system, or transmitted in any form or by any means—electronic, mechanical, photocopying, recording, or otherwise—without the prior written permission of Lerner Publishing Group, Inc., except for the inclusion of brief quotations in an acknowledged review.

Darby Creek
A division of Lerner Publishing Group, Inc.
241 First Avenue North
Minneapolis, MN 55401 USA

For reading levels and more information, look up this title at
www.lernerbooks.com.

The images in this book are used with the permission of: © iStockphoto. com/VeryOlive (teen girl); © iStockphoto.com/CollinsChin (background); © iStockphoto.com/mart_m (dog tags).

Main body text set in Janson Text LT Std 12/17.5.
Typeface provided by Adobe Systems.

Library of Congress Cataloging-in-Publication Data

The Cataloging-in-Publication Data for *Freedom Flight* is on file at the Library of Congress.
ISBN 978-1-4677-8051-3 (lib. bdg.)
ISBN 978-1-4677-8092-6 (pbk.)
ISBN 978-1-4677-8819-9 (EB pdf)

Manufactured in the United States of America
1 – SB – 7/15/15

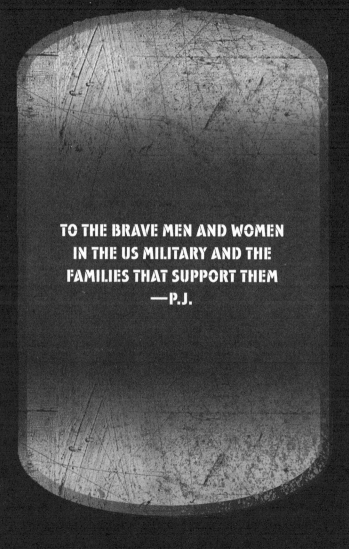

TO THE BRAVE MEN AND WOMEN
IN THE US MILITARY AND THE
FAMILIES THAT SUPPORT THEM
—P.J.

0

"I'm calling it her freedom flight," Paige Harkins whispered to Josie Wilkins, mouth barely moving as she uncharacteristically broke cadet rules. They stood together, along with their friend Erin and other members of the Sam Houston High ROTC unit, on the hot pavement at Lackland base in San Antonio, Texas.

Despite the heat, it was as if the young men and women were frozen as they stood staring at their commander. Other than Paige's whisper, the only sound was the flapping of American flags in a non-cooling breeze.

Beads of sweat trickled from under the brim of Josie's cap onto her neatly pressed blue uniform that was identical to that of the other Air Force Junior Reserve Officer Training Corps cadets. Paige thought Josie was sweating because she was undisciplined and carrying too much weight for a cadet. No one in Paige's unit, school, or family would ever accuse Paige of that.

Paige squinted, the blazing sun in her eyes. For the other cadets this was another AFJROTC outing, another chance to display the colors and show off the unit's discipline. But for Paige, it was more, much more. It was the moment she'd been expecting for years. Her mom. Home. Not for twelve months before being deployed again, but for good. For great.

On the plane that towered over them were members of the 455th Air Expeditionary Wing. The unit had been activated in 2002, just two years after Paige was born in a hospital in Germany. Since then, the unit had been assigned to Afghanistan. As hot as the pavement was in Texas, Paige guessed it was nothing like the heat of Bagram Airfield, where her mom had been stationed many times over the years.

"March!" Commander Eckert yelled. As always, the cadets did exactly as ordered. The unit moved closer as the staircase from the large Air Force plane was deployed.

"Attention!"

Right hands moved quickly from the cadets' sides to their foreheads as they saluted the plane. Paige closed her eyes, telling herself it was the exhaust from the plane that was making them water. Telling herself she wouldn't cry. Cadets didn't cry. Soldiers didn't cry. They live. They die. They fight, so Paige fought back tears as she waited for her mom to emerge.

One by one, members of the unit exited the plane until, at the top of the stairs, ramrod straight as if at attention, Paige's mother stood.

Paige expected to see a smile on her face and it was there, but it passed quickly. Her mom's eyes narrowed, her lips tightened.

As her mom walked slowly down the stairs, clutching the railing, Paige tried to concentrate on the scene in front of her and not let her mind drift to a dark place. Another plane landing, another return home. She hadn't been there for it since she was only three at the time. Her mom wouldn't speak of it. Paige could beg, bargain, or bray, but her mother was unbending in her silence about Paige's dad's return from Iraq. His flight had stopped first at the Dover Air Force Base in Delaware. There, Air Force Captain Roger Harkins came off the plane in a flag-draped casket.

2

SEPTEMBER 27 / SUNDAY AFTERNOON
NINA'S CANTINA

"It's just a glass of wine," Paige said to her mother, feeling oddly defensive.

"You're fifteen," her mom barked. "You're not old enough to drink."

Paige and her mom's terse conversation could barely be heard over the laughter coming from the extended members of Paige's family. From as far away as Houston, Paige's aunts, uncles, nieces, and nephews had ventured to San Antonio to welcome Capt. Harkins home.

"So raise your glasses," Paige's Uncle Jacob, her mom's older brother, said. Paige and her older brother Perry had lived with Uncle Jacob and Aunt Tracy whenever their career military mom was deployed. Paige's mom glared at Paige until she returned the wine glass to the table.

"It's great to have you home, Helen," Aunt Tracy said. Everybody yelled in agreement, but none louder than Paige in the crowded party room at Nina's Cantina.

Once the eating and drinking were finished, everyone gathered for pictures. Paige photo-bombed almost every shot with her mom until it became a joke.

"Paige, people will think you're a conjoined twin or something attached to Mom's shoulder," Perry shouted.

Paige's mom kept smiling for photos, until someone hugged her too tightly. The open eyes and wide smile were quickly replaced by a mask of pain. "Perry, get me a chair," her mom said.

"Are you okay, Mom?" Paige asked.

"I'm just tired," her mom said, and then sighed. "It's a long flight."

"But it's your last one, right?" Paige asked. She knew the answer but wanted to hear the words from her mom's mouth. "It was your freedom flight."

"Not really, that's what they call the last flight when you retire," her mom said. "I've got a few more years, but I hope all of them will be here at home with my family."

Perry picked up a chair, carrying it over his head like he was lifting weights. "Make room," Perry said. At six-foot-two and 210 pounds, Perry could easily get everyone to clear a path for him.

"Thanks, Pretty," Paige's mom said. Perry blushed at his childhood nickname. Paige's mom eased into the faded green and white chair. "I just can't stand like that for too long."

Paige helped her mom into the chair. "Thanks, Pug." Paige winced at her childish nickname, her mispronouncing of her own name. It seemed cute at one time, but now, not at all.

"Helen, what are your plans?" Aunt Tracy asked. Distracted by her phone, Paige didn't catch other questions people asked. It was a text from David, her boyfriend. She had wanted to invite him but was told that her mother wanted the party limited to family only.

Paige's mom started to answer about her return to duty at Lackland but stopped in mid-sentence. In the middle of typing her reply to David, Paige felt eyes upon her. She looked up from her phone, from David, to see her mother staring at her. A stare as cold as the day was hot.

"Turn it off, Pug," her mom snapped, like an order to one of the soldiers who had been under her command. In a flash, Paige complied. She knew that was what she did best.

3

"Where's Mom?" Perry asked Paige as he finished his third bowl of cornflakes.

Paige shrugged her shoulders. "Still on Afghan time, I guess."

"I think she's still sleeping," Aunt Tracy said as she walked into the room. Uncle Jacob had left for work early, so the coffee was ready to go. Paige liked her sugar with a little coffee.

"That's all she's done since she got home." Paige poured coffee into a Texas A&M mug.

She tried to recall details about the last time her mom was home, but they all ran together in her head like some music video. Still, something seemed different this time.

"It will take time to adjust," Aunt Tracy said, passing Paige the sugar. "It always does. That's why we wanted all of you to stay here for a week before moving back into your house. Gives your uncle a chance to go see if everything's okay since the renters moved out, too."

"I think it gets harder, having her home," Paige said as she tugged at her San Antonio Spurs T-shirt. "I thought it would get easier, but it's the opposite. I was too young to know better the other times."

"Except this time is the last time," Aunt Tracy said, kissing Paige on top of her head. "I'm going to miss the two of you. That's for sure. Not that we see much of either of you anymore."

Paige laughed. With her sophomore year starting, it seemed she was never at home because of David, ROTC, running cross-country, and keeping up with her wide circle of friends from all over the world at all hours. Her neighborhood near the base in a military town like San Antonio was home to a few, but for most it was a two-year stop on the road to somewhere else.

"I got some of my college buds coming this weekend to load up our stuff from here and help us move back home," Perry said. Perry was a senior at Texas A&M at San Antonio and in the college ROTC program. He'd graduate with a degree in civil engineering and then start his commitment to the Air Force. Paige thought it odd that just as her mother was coming home, her brother was going away after this school year.

"David said he could help us move, too," Paige said as she stirred the sugar into her coffee. That was David Garcia: the sweetness in a dark, bitter life filled with loss, loneliness, and longing.

"We'll be lifting boxes, not writing poetry," Perry said. Paige let it go. There was no use fighting with Perry about David or anything else, since Perry was never wrong. Just ask him.

"I need to get ready for school," Paige said, taking her coffee but no breakfast back toward her room on the second floor of the old house. The stairs creaked, so Paige walked softly as she climbed them, not wanting to wake her mother. She deserved her sleep, her time alone.

They'd have plenty of time together, especially once Perry went off to officer school next summer.

In her room, Paige mulled over what to wear. Like many military brat girls, she'd been quite the tomboy, but that had changed over the past year as her body changed. Paige couldn't help but notice the attention she got now from boys—first Travis, then others, and now David.

Just as Paige settled in front of the mirror to fix her hair, she heard her mother's bedroom door open and close. Then steps—slow ones. The bathroom door opened but didn't close. Then another sound, a thump like somebody dropping books on the floor at school.

"Paige." It was her mom's voice, faint, yet

somehow pleading. "Pug, are you there?"

Paige raced from her chair, out the door, and toward the bathroom. Her mom lay on the floor, clutching her back. Her T-shirt was pushed up so Paige could see the scars from the back surgery she'd had more than two years ago when the medevac helicopter she was in got shot down. After the crash, they said her mom wouldn't walk when she started rehab at a hospital in Germany. But she walked, first with a walker, then a cane, then on her own. While she could have left the service, she stayed on, though she traded her place piloting a Chinook chopper for sitting behind a desk. She had been proud to be redeployed. But now she was on the bathroom floor, writhing in pain.

"In my room, top drawer of the dresser. Bring the bottle of small white pills," she said. More like a sprinter than a distance runner, Paige raced toward her mom's room, found the drawer and the bottle. When she returned, Aunt Tracy was on the floor next to her mom.

"Mom, what's wrong?" Paige asked and she fumbled to open the bottle. Her mother ripped it from her hands, pulled the lid off with her teeth, and dumped several pills into the palm of her left hand. Then she put the cap back on the bottle and dropped it on the bathroom floor where it tipped over and rolled toward Paige. White pills. Orange bottle. White label. Black letters. One word: OxyContin.

4

OCTOBER 2 / FRIDAY MORNING
SAM HOUSTON HIGH SCHOOL PARKING LOT

"Dismissed!" Commander Eckert yelled with the same intensity as when he yelled "Attention" at the start of drills. Every Friday before school, during zero hour, the cadets practiced a demonstration for the upcoming Veterans Day parade. They'd be the lead ROTC unit.

"That man will be the death of me," Josie sighed. Paige laughed.

"That's what commanders do: kill people," added Erin Collins, a sophomore like Josie and

15

Paige. Paige wondered how she could have so much bitterness in her voice this early.

"Then why don't you just quit?" Paige asked.

"I can't, you can't, none of us can," Erin said. Like Paige, Erin had lost a parent in Afghanistan. Her mom, an Air Force medic. Josie's dad had suffered really serious injuries. But death and destruction brought the girls together, and ROTC bound them. Like David, they stayed strong while others broke.

Paige didn't argue in a fight she couldn't win. "So about Homecoming?" Paige asked.

The three girls talked over each other as they discussed the upcoming event, which all planned to attend for the first time. Alonzo, a junior also in ROTC, was taking Josie while Erin was going with Blake, an older guy she knew from her church youth group.

"My mom's taking me shopping for my dress," Paige said.

"I thought we were going to go together," Josie asked. Paige looked at the pavement.

"Come on, Josie, her mom just got back stateside," Erin said. "I always thought I'd go shopping for dresses for Homecoming, prom, and wedding with my mom, but . . ."

"Don't give up, Erin," Paige said. "Maybe your dad will remarry."

"If he does, so what?" Erin countered. "That will be his wife but not my mom. Paige, you don't know how lucky you are that your mom made it through and she's back home."

Paige nodded and smiled, even as dark thoughts overcame her. Which mom? The mom that left before this last deployment? The one that came home two weeks ago? The mom who was on Paige's back from after school until early evening? Or the mom who lay on the floor of the bathroom writhing in agony until she downed her pills? Erin had one dad; Paige had four moms.

"Ready?"

Paige felt David's hand on her shoulder. She turned, kissed him on the cheek, and wrapped herself around his long right arm. As tall as Paige's brother but as skinny as a flagpole, David seemed stronger to Paige than anyone she knew. Both of his parents died in the war, serving in the Army, yet he'd never wavered in his commitment to serve his country.

"So, my Aunt Lita thought maybe you and your mom could come over for dinner soon," David said. "She's been back two weeks and I haven't met her. Are you embarrassed—"

"She's just busy, settling in her new job at Lackland," Paige interrupted nervously.

"That's the thing I don't get and I don't think anyone can understand until it happens to them," David said. "One day, you're putting your life on the line and then a couple weeks later you're sitting behind a desk reading reports or whatever it is your mom does."

"I don't know what she does," Paige admitted. "She doesn't talk about it. She never talked about what she did when deployed, but that's because she didn't want me to be scared."

"They can't know what it's like, most of them." David pointed at a group hanging out near the back doors: stoners, wanna-be bangers, and other troublemakers to be avoided.

"What do you mean, David?"

"To go to bed every night wondering if in the middle of the night the call is going to come," David said. "Or in the morning, two messengers in dress uniform outside your front door. You invite strangers in to give you the news you're prepared for but still can't handle."

Paige grabbed onto David's arm. She felt it shaking and his tears falling on her shoulder.

5

"Why are these dishes not put away?" Paige's mom snapped. Before Paige had time to answer, her mother continued her post-dinner rant. "Is this how Aunt Tracy let you live?"

"I'll do it after my homework," Paige said softly, as if that would lower her mom's voice.

"You'll do it now!" her mom barked in a tone fitting ROTC Commander Eckert.

Paige stopped the urge to salute her mom—a sarcastic act of obedience and defiance—and did as she was told. She didn't ask why Perry wasn't asked to help or why he didn't seem to suffer under the increasingly harsh lash of her mother's post-work tongue.

"I want this house spotless, or is that too much to ask?" Paige's mom continued. They stood in the kitchen. In the living room, Perry watched football on TV and talked on the phone. "I had to live in the worst possible places with rockets being fired at me, so now that I'm in my home, it's going to be perfect. Do you understand me, Pug?" Paige simply nodded. "I can't believe Tracy let you live like this."

Paige looked around the small kitchen. Except for the clean dishes in the dishwasher, it was spotless. What was her mom talking about? She had thought that once they had gotten so much unpacked over the weekend her mom might lay off and relax.

"I just have other things to do after school," Paige countered.

"There's nothing more important than

your family."

Paige shook her head like she'd been slapped. She wondered how such a small task had suddenly turned into such a big issue.

"Maybe when you're home, safe in your bed, you don't know that, but when you've—"

Paige didn't want to hear another lecture. "Are we going dress shopping tomorrow?"

"You're not going to any dance with anyone until I meet him."

Paige started to remind her mom that she was supposed to meet David just yesterday when he'd come over to study with Paige. Instead, her mom had been asleep by eight. That was her mom's pattern: a monster to Paige from the time she got home from work until after dinner and then behind her closed bedroom door until morning.

"You'll like him, I know it." Paige didn't know anyone who didn't like David. Smart and good looking, but not too much so.

"At fifteen you shouldn't even have a boyfriend."

Paige answered by opening the dishwasher. Everything neat and organized, just like her mother liked it. Forks, knives, and spoons standing at attention. Good silver soldiers.

"It can't lead to anything but trouble."

Noticing her mom standing by the cabinet where they stored the coffee mugs, Paige handed her the Texas A&M mug. Taking it in her hand, her mom turned to open the cabinet and suddenly jerked and yelled in pain. The mug slipped from her hand and smashed onto the kitchen floor, shattering into small pieces. Without apologizing, she told Paige, "Get a broom." She clutched the counter.

Doing as she was told, Paige found the broom and swept up the mess. Her mom, her hand on her back, started out of the kitchen toward her room. No doubt toward her pills. As Paige dumped the small white pieces of china into the trash can, she knew soon her mom would dump small white pills into her hand. Her mom's words echoed in her head—*It can't lead to anything but trouble.*

6

"Sprichst Du Deutsch?" Paige asked a befuddled Blake. His girlfriend Erin laughed.

"Nihongo o hanashimasu ka?" Josie asked in Japanese.

Like a rehearsal for the dinner before the Homecoming dance, Paige sat with her friends and their boyfriends around a large table at a crowded Starbucks on Saturday night. Only David, who was at a weekend church retreat, couldn't join them. But Paige kept in constant touch via text. It was yet another language she'd mastered.

"You're speaking in tongues," Blake laughed.

"When you're a military brat, you learn the language or else," Josie said. Josie's parents were both career military and had moved around the globe, while Paige had only spent her short time in Germany. She later learned a little German and liked to show off when she could.

"And that's what all of you are going to do, join the military?" Blake said. Like they were performing, the three girls and Alonzo nodded their heads in unison. "I just don't get it."

"Blake, you don't get wanting to serve your country?" Erin sounded peeved.

"No, I get wanting to serve," Blake said, his foot firmly entrenched in his mouth. "Just, I know how the wars have affected your family members. I mean, aren't you afraid of that?"

The girls looked at each other, back and forth, as if deciding who should strike first. "You can't be afraid to die," Josie said. "You can't be afraid of paying the ultimate price."

"No, I mean, aren't you afraid of what happens to those who love you," Blake said. He squeezed Erin's left hand. Erin blushed, Josie laughed, and Alonzo looked embarrassed.

"You accept the risks," Paige said softly. "You accept the consequences."

While her words didn't silence the room, they did silence those at the table. Perhaps realizing his mistake, Blake excused himself to go get another cookie. Josie nudged Alonzo to join him.

Once the girls were alone, Erin apologized. "Sorry, Blake just doesn't get it," she said.

"It's like speaking another language," Josie added.

"I'm doing that now," Paige said, placing her phone face down on the table.

"Texting isn't a language," Erin said, and then laughed. "Maybe sexting is, but . . ."

With no smile on her face, Paige cut her off. "I mean at home," she said.

The noise in Starbucks seemed to grow louder as Paige's table fell silent. "Everything okay?" Erin finally asked. "I mean, you were so excited about your mom coming home for good."

Paige started to speak but hesitated, sipping her drink to stall for time. If she would tell anyone, it would be her best friends, but she didn't know what, or how much, to reveal. Her mom seemed sometimes in more pain than she remembered but also a lot more distant. When she'd been home before, they'd spent lots of time together, but this time, Paige saw more of her mom's closed bedroom door than she did of her face.

"You know you can tell us anything," Josie said. A hundred secrets shared among them marched in Paige's memory. Nights spent laughing about stupid things during the school day; other nights spent crying about their parents. "Paige, what's wrong?"

"I don't know," Paige said. "I don't know if I'm the problem or she's the problem."

"Give it time." Josie covered Paige's outstretched hands. Erin put her hands on top.

"You've changed since she left," Erin said and then giggled like they had in middle school.

"She still wants me to be Pug and my brother to be Pretty," Paige said. "And I want her to be—" Her phone buzzed. She picked it up. A text from David, who just wanted her to be Paige.

". . . the same mom who you remember from when you were little," Josie finished for her.

7

OCTOBER 11 / SUNDAY AFTERNOON
SOUTH PARK MALL

"I don't think so," Paige's mom said, shaking her head. She sat outside the dressing room at Macy's in the South Park Mall on Military Drive. She'd vetoed all of Paige's Homecoming dress choices in other stores. They were running out of mall.

Paige sighed, turned, and looked in the mirror again. "There's nothing wrong with it."

In the mirror, Paige saw the pained look on her mother's face. It fit: her mom might be in pain, but she also was a pain and a handful of pills wasn't going to change that fact any time soon. Paige wanted to ask her mom about the pills but couldn't think of a way to frame the question that didn't sound disrespectful. Was she this way last time she was home? Paige didn't think so, but she couldn't remember, or maybe she just hadn't been paying attention.

"It's too low cut," Paige's mom finally answered. It was one of her favorite answers.

"Maybe I should just wear my ROTC uniform," Paige said through tight lips, still looking in the mirror. She remembered her mom's comment on her lip gloss: "Too shiny."

"Maybe you just won't go to Homecoming," her mom quickly countered. "I still haven't met this guy."

Paige pivoted quickly, without pain. "That's not my fault! I tried—" she stopped herself from making a snarky comment about her mom's weird sleep patterns. "Anyway, Aunt Tracy let me go shopping with my friends."

Paige's mom twisted in the hard chair. "I'm not your Aunt Tracy."

Taking a step forward, Paige said into the floor beneath her. "No, you're not."

Loud music, louder voices, and the ringing of cash registers filled the silence after Paige spoke.

Paige's mom crossed her arms. "Try another dress."

As if in formation, Paige's right hand shot up toward her forehead. "Yes sir."

"That's enough of that." Her mom started to stand but quickly sank back down. "I've got quite enough to do without having to pick out clothes for you, Pug, since you can't be trusted not to dress like—"

"Paige, not Pug." Hard. Defiant. Followed by a hard stare. But then Paige broke the stare when she saw the hurt in her mom's eyes, coming from more than her back, Paige guessed.

"Mom, I'm not a kid anymore," Paige said softly.

"No, you're not," her mom said just as softly. "I

31

can see that." Paige felt like her mom was assessing her body like the guys did at school. While she normally hid her curves under her uniform and Perry's hand-me-downs, Paige wanted something special for Homecoming, something adult.

Paige paused, unsure what to say or do. Her mother had surrendered, at least in this battle. Should she pick another fight or accept her mom's terms? "I'll try another dress," Paige said.

"Maybe something in blue."

"Maybe."

Paige wandered around the store, avoiding her mom, avoiding another confrontation. She gazed with envy at groups of girls she knew from school, shopping together and laughing. When she saw moms and daughters talking, not fighting, the envy overtook her like a tidal wave. Paige picked five more dresses, four of which she guessed her mom would hate ("Really Paige, show some modesty") so she'd have to accept the fifth: a strapless dress that was Air Force blue.

When Paige returned to the dressing room

area, her mom was gone. Paige thought it was odd but went inside to try on the dress. She texted pictures of each of them to Josie and Erin. Since her mom still wasn't back, Paige sat in the dressing room texting with her friends. The vote for the blue dress was unanimous. Paige slipped it on again and gazed in the mirror. She loved it, her friends loved it, and so would David. Their opinion mattered more than her mom's. They knew Paige in the now, not in the past.

"Mom? This is the—" Paige started talking as she stepped out of the dressing room and turned where she hoped her mother would be seated. "Mom?"

Paige's mom didn't respond. Instead, she sat in the chair, head down, fast asleep. But not actually asleep, Paige knew—just passed out from pain meds.

Turning back to her dressing room, Paige thought bitterly about how her mom escaped bad dreams and memories by passing out, only to cause nightmares for the ones still awake.

8

"I never thought I'd feel this way," Paige confessed to her brother. They sat in the living room. Paige balanced her phone on one leg, her algebra book on the other. Perry drank an oversized Mountain Dew and watched ESPN with the volume muted.

"Mom's just getting used to the house again. Throw all your girly stuff around in your room if you want to make a mess to make it feel homey," Perry said.

"That's not what I'm talking about," Paige said. She slammed her book shut, but Perry didn't take that as a sign to turn off the TV. "I mean I actually dread her coming home."

"Hey, inspections, cadet. Get used to them."

Paige tapped her foot nervously. Paige and Perry were brother and sister, not friends. With six years difference in their ages and even more in experiences growing up, Paige loved her brother, but had never felt tight with him. Unlike their mom, he was always in close physical proximity . . . but he was never emotionally close. Perry was a proud, stand-tall, stand-alone Texas man. Especially when in uniform, Perry looked a lot like their father in the few pictures still around.

Paige glanced around the room. Everything was in place here and in the rest of house. With her mom's back pain, all household chores fell to Paige. She'd quit cross-country—one of the few things she'd ever quit—to help out around the house. Running she would give up, but ROTC marching, never. She still hadn't told her aunt and uncle about cross-country, though.

"It's more than that, Perry."

Perry nodded, smiled, and then reacted to the game on ESPN, not Paige.

"I'm worried about her," Paige said, as she ran her fingers nervously through her hair.

"She's fine, Paige. You worry too much," Perry said, sounding bored. "We've been through this how many times? She comes home, it takes a while, but we readjust."

"It's different this time," Paige said.

Her mom had been hurt two years ago, but Paige mostly remembered her mom's fight to recover. Once she'd exceeded the doctors' predictions, Paige thought everything was going to be fine and her mom would just get better and better. She had hardly even been aware of her mom using pain meds before. Had her mom always been affected like this by them, and Paige had just been too young to tell? Or had her injuries gotten worse again? Or was it something else?

"She's adjusting to civilian life," Perry said. "When she was deployed, she had to be on edge all the time. You never knew if your number was coming up. A shell shot into the base. A mortar fired at your helicopter. An Afghan guy you trained to protect you turning his weapon on you. Now, she sits in an office reading reports or something. It would change you too."

"How do you know this?"

"She told me."

"Why didn't she tell me?" Paige asked the question out loud, but it was mostly to herself.

Perry shrugged, readjusted his place on the sofa, and leaned toward the TV screen. "I don't know, Pug, did you ever ask her?"

Paige fingered her algebra book. Simple problems, simple answers. This was hard. "I'm worried about her using all those pain meds."

Perry remained focus on the TV. "She got wounded and the meds are helping her."

"It's worse than before."

"Just shut up about it," Perry said. "Nobody

knows and you need to keep it that way."

Perry unmuted the TV. A team must have scored a touchdown—from the TV came the loud roar of the crowd, loud enough to cover Perry's silence, Paige's tears, and the sound of the front door opening.

Mom was home, Paige knew. *It's what I always wanted*, she thought, *until I got it.*

9

OCTOBER 16 / FRIDAY EARLY EVENING
JACOB AND TRACY ALEXANDER'S HOUSE

"It was probably an old Russian SAM," Paige's mom said. David had asked her if she'd been wounded in battle. Paige hated the story more every time she heard it. The first time all she felt was fear at how close her mother came to dying, but now she resented how the injury from the crash kept her mom from living fully.

Paige, Perry, her mom, and David sat around the dinner table at Uncle Jacob and

Aunt Tracy's house. Never knowing which Capt. Harkins would show up, Paige thought her mom's first meeting with David should include reinforcements. Especially since tomorrow was Homecoming.

"That couldn't have been your only one," David said. Polite. Measured. David.

"One time, this was back in '07 . . ." And Paige's mom told a story she'd never heard before about another close call on a training mission. Paige shifted in her chair with a pained expression on her face, noticing a similar look on her mom. That meant she was in pain rather than on pain meds, at least. Paige's mom kept twisting her body in her chair and spewing stories, maybe to distract herself.

In a small voice, Paige asked aloud, "Mom, why didn't you tell me this before?"

Paige's question rattled her mom, and as she fished for an answer, Perry spoke up.

"Because, Pug, you were a child and children don't need to know this stuff."

"Correct, Perry," Paige's mom said.

"A friend of mine who grew up in Killeen near Fort Hood told me this story." Perry sipped from a bottle of Lone Star beer. "One of the teachers thought it would be a good idea to honor the parents who died. So she put up an American flag sticker on this wipe board every time she heard that a student had lost a parent. Pretty soon she was on her second wipe board. That board had more stickers than the flag had stars. Wish you had gone to that school, Pug?"

"Weren't your parents at Fort Hood, David?" Uncle Jacob said.

"Yeah," David said. "Both of my folks were infantry," he told Paige's mom. "One died in Iraq, the other in Afghanistan. Everybody I knew lost somebody. We became instant friends."

"Shared loss brings people together," Aunt Tracy said.

"I think I became friends with everybody who lost a parent like I did," David said. "The schools in Killeen did a good job helping us through it, but you never get over it."

Paige started to speak but instead joined in the silence which had overtaken the room.

"I was glad that when my aunt and uncle moved that we came here and I could meet other military kids who could relate," David added.

"Well, David, you certainly are a fine young man," Paige's mom said. Paige tried to mask her sigh of relief. "Polite and willing to listen."

Paige's head snapped back: those words seemed directed at her. She wanted to say something but didn't have a chance while her mom asked David more questions about his parents, growing up without them, and everything else. Like she was debriefing after a mission.

When David talked about his father's funeral, he started to cry. Paige could tell her mom's pained expression wasn't just about her back—his crying was an affront to her.

"What about Dad's funeral?" Paige asked, feeling defiant but also wanting to save David from embarrassing himself. "You've never talked about it, Mom." The room silenced again. Paige's mom stared at her like a sniper.

"So about the Homecoming dance," was Paige's mom's non-answer. "I expect you to bring Paige home on time. No drinking, no drugs, no funny business. Understand, Mr. Garcia?"

David nodded while Paige covered her face.

"You can trust me, Capt. Harkins," David said. Paige liked how he used her rank.

Unlike Josie and Erin, Paige held no high expectations for Homecoming. She'd already expected too much from one homecoming and been nothing but disappointed. *How about no drugs yourself,* Paige thought, but said nothing. The conversation resumed about the wars, but nothing was said about her dad's funeral. Like it was classified information.

10

"You're late," Paige's mom said the second Paige walked in the door, exactly four minutes and forty seconds past her midnight curfew for Homecoming. Her mom sat clear-eyed with gritted teeth on a hard kitchen chair. Paige thought she looked more like a rodeo bull about to charge than her mother.

"It's not my fault," Paige said. "Blake and Erin had a fight and—"

"I don't want to hear it," her mom said. "I don't want to hear your lies."

"I'm not lying!" Paige shouted.

"Lower your voice."

Paige held her phone in front of her. "Call Erin, she'll tell you. Call David, he—"

"I might well be calling David, or at least his aunt."

"What are you talking about?"

"Come closer!" Paige's mother ordered. Paige hesitated. "Now!"

Paige took off her heels—her ROTC marching boots caused less pain—and stepped forward. Like she was in line for inspection, her mother's eyes examined every inch of her.

"Your dress is wrinkled."

Paige tried not to blush. While they'd slipped away a few times during the dance to make out, that was it, thanks to David. Like many students at their school, David took his religion very seriously. It wasn't something he just said on Sunday. He lived it every day.

"It seems like you took it off—or maybe David took it off—and put it back on."

The pink blush on Paige's face slowly turned to red anger. "That didn't happen."

"Don't lie to me, Pug," her mom snapped. "I was a teenager too."

"If I'm a teenager, then don't call me Pug like I was child or a dog or a pet or—"

"You don't tell me what to do," her mom said. "You understand that, Pug?"

Paige balled her fists by her side. She wanted to march into her mom's room, grab a handful of pills, and shut her up. Paige knew her mom was in pain; she didn't know why her mom felt the need to take it out on her. "I'm going to bed."

"Again, you mean."

Paige shook her head but said nothing as she turned toward her room.

"I'm not done inspecting you, cadet," her mom shouted after her. "Maybe I'll need to inspect you everywhere."

Paige knew what that meant. She pivoted,

narrowed her eyes, and yanked off her dress. Her mother stayed seated in the hard chair, her shoulders twitching while Paige stood in front of her in her underwear. "I don't know what you think you're even looking for, but see, Ma, no hickies. Why don't you just trust me?"

"Because of your father," her mom whispered just loud enough for Paige to hear. The pain in her mom's face seemed to drain out of her. "I'm the reason he's dead."

"What are you talking about?" Paige walked back to her mom. She knelt by the chair.

"We were still in high school when Perry was born. You knew that," her mom said.

While much of Paige's family history went unspoken, she could do the math. Perry was twenty-one; her mom would turn thirty-nine next month. "Both of our parents, well, they were no help."

Paige never asked why her grandparents hadn't been part of her life. She accepted it.

"So, there we were, young, no money, and

a baby," her mom said softly. "So we joined the Air National Guard at first. It seemed like an easy answer. A few years of commitment, a steady paycheck, a chance at college. We didn't really intend to stay in so long. But we couldn't have known what was coming. We started with just weekends on a base and we liked being military. Then just when life seemed good, we found ourselves overseas in combat."

Paige closed her eyes tight as her mom continued taking blame for her dad's death.

"If I would've been strong, I wouldn't have got pregnant and we would've lived different lives. Your father would be here today and I'd be in one piece instead of a crippled wreck." Paige's mother's voice shook almost as much as her hands.

00

"Is there anything I can say?" Paige asked Erin. Erin had missed school Monday, and from her fragile emotional state, Paige wondered if she should have stayed home today, too.

"No, nothing. Blake said it all."

Josie sat on the other side of Erin. Paige had asked David and Alonzo not to join them for lunch, not only so the three could talk about Erin and Blake breaking up, but because seeing other couples, Paige knew, would make Erin feel worse.

"I'm sorry, but he was too old for you," Josie said softly. "What was he, nineteen?"

"He just turned eighteen," Erin answered. "That was the problem."

"So what happened?" Paige asked. At the Homecoming dance, the two had left the group, but only Erin returned to the table. When she did, tears were running down her face. Paige shuddered at the thought of her and David breaking up. It would be more hurt than she could stand.

"If he did something to you, I will personally punch his lights out," Josie slammed her right fist into left hand. Paige laughed but felt bad when she saw Erin's hurt expression.

"It's not what he did," Erin whispered. "It's what he didn't do."

Paige and Jose exchanged confused glances. Finally Paige spoke. "I don't understand."

"When you turn eighteen," Erin said. "You

need to register for selective service, and he said he didn't want to do it. He said he wasn't going to die or get his legs blown off for his country like some fool."

"I will seriously hurt him," Josie said.

"Then he said that all those people who died in Iraq and Afghanistan were fools," Erin continued. "Dying in some foreign country and now look at them both, falling into chaos."

Paige nodded. She'd overheard Uncle Jacob and Aunt Tracy express similar ideas. To them, the purpose of the military was to defend the homeland, but nothing more.

"And then we just got into it about everything," Erin said. "And now it's over."

"He's a jerk," Josie said. "My dad wasn't injured for nothing."

Paige put her arm around Erin's shaking shoulders. Paige never thought about what her dad's death meant—she was so young when it happened. He was dead. Where and why and how never mattered. Dead was dead; thinking about it changed nothing, but still she yearned to know more. Air Force fatality numbers were low compared to other branches—maybe there was something weird about his death.

"I should've known," Erin said. "Blake never came to our ROTC events. He never said anything about it. I thought because we went to the same church, we believed the same things."

"If I see him, I'm giving an attitude adjustment," Josie said, half laughing, half serious.

As Josie tried to console Erin, Paige found herself distracted by the controlled chaos that was the cafeteria at lunchtime. It was a diverse high school, yet the white kids mostly hung with other white kids, and the black, Hispanic, and Asian kids also hung with their own kind and apart from others. Race-related fights were a normal occurrence in the factionalized school, except on the integrated ROTC squad. There the only color that mattered was Air Force blue.

"I miss him," Erin said. "And I hate him. I don't know what to think anymore."

Paige shrugged in agreement, not thinking about Blake and Erin, but about her and her mom. She missed the mom she wanted and sometimes hated the one she had. That's what made the military so attractive to Paige: it was black and white, right and wrong, salute and obey.

"It hurts so much," Erin said, holding back tears. "I just want not to hurt."

Paige clutched Erin's hand, but her mom's drugged-out stupor invaded Paige's mind. *If I hurt as bad as my mom must*, Paige thought, *wouldn't I do the same things?*

12

"Mom, is that you?" Paige asked the figure in her bedroom doorway. The door cracked open further, letting in a beam of light. It hadn't woken her; she'd spent most of the night imagining her dark thoughts if she broke up with David like Erin had with Blake.

"What time are we leaving?" Paige's mom said, her voice sounding almost totally alien.

Paige sat up in bed and blocked out the light

with her right hand. "Leaving?"

"1400 hours," Paige's mom mumbled.

"Mom, what are you talking about?" Paige asked, but her mom didn't answer. The door shut and Paige heard footsteps walking toward the living room. Paige yawned, stretched, and climbed out of bed. She checked her phone: 4 a.m. She needed to be at ROTC practice in two hours, all the while running on no sleep. She followed her mom, as silent as a shadow.

In the living room, her mom lay on the couch, phone in her hand. The only light in the room came from the phone and the streetlights piercing the darkness. "Mom, are you okay?"

"I just miss you, that's all," Paige's mom mumbled. Paige thought it sounded like her mom's lips had swelled shut over her mouth. "It won't be long until we're together again."

Paige wondered if she should shake her mother awake. She didn't know if she was sleep-walking, dreaming, or what was happening. Paige knew one thing for sure: she was scared.

Her mom had changed from when she was home last, but Paige didn't know why. Had she gotten hurt again? Last time her mom was home she was her mom; this time she wasn't the same woman. It was like the Mom that went away last stayed overseas and this new Mom came home.

"I can't wait to see you either," her mom mumbled.

Paige sighed. She was sad, angry, and confused, but mostly she was determined to figure out what was going on. Who was her mother talking to? Paige left the living room and walked softly on the creaky floors into her mom's room. She opened the top drawer where she'd found the pills before and found . . . nothing.

Paige moved next to the small dresser by the bed. There was an open can of Lone Star Light on top and Paige picked it up. It seemed about half empty, half full. Whatever. She flicked on the small lamp on the dresser and opened the top drawer.

It was October, but not yet Halloween,

except in her mother's room. Pills, like holiday candy, filled the drawer. Some were in bottles, some loose. Paige picked up the bottles: different shapes, different sizes, some heavy, some light. OxyContin. Valium.

For a second, Paige felt like snatching all the pills and flushing them down the toilet. Just as quickly, she suddenly wanted to grab a handful, wake up her mother, and swallow them all in front of her. Let her see what it looked like to have a zombie instead of a family member in the house.

Then she heard it, from the other room: laughter. Laughter like she'd not heard from her mom since she had returned. Not loud or drunken, not enough to wake Perry, but laughter nonetheless. Paige pushed in the drawer, flicked off the light, and returned to the living room. Her mom lay on the sofa, her eyes almost rolling back in her head, but her hand still clutching the phone. "No, you say it first," her mom said into the phone, her voice heavy.

Silence. Paige couldn't hear the voice on the other end.

"I love you, too, Captain," her mom said. "Come home safe. I miss you."

Who? What? Paige felt her knees buckle. Was she dreaming?

Kneeling next to the sofa, Paige listened as her mother repeated those same words over and over until the phone fell from her hand. Paige picked up the phone and looked at the last number dialed. Voicemail. She stuffed the phone under her Spurs T-shirt and walked into the kitchen. She dialed the number but couldn't figure out the voicemail password. Who was she calling at two in the morning? Who was the captain her mom was talking to? Did she have a new boyfriend? Paige pinched herself; she was wide awake, but her mom was passed out cold.

13

"Do it again, cadets!" Commander Eckert shouted. Paige thought the rumble of thunder in the background made him sound like the voice of a very angry God. Maybe it was lack of sleep, the distraction of Erin's inability to focus, or the steady cold rain, but the unit wasn't functioning. "We only have a few weeks to get this right and you will get it right!" the commander continued.

The Sam Houston High unit had been selected to be the lead ROTC unit in the San Antonio Veterans Day parade, one of the biggest in the state of Texas. But if the unit didn't follow orders, Paige thought it would turn into one of the biggest embarrassments in her life.

"Harkins, get with it!" squad leader Brad Richardson shouted. He always shouted.

Paige nodded, tried to focus, but her feet wouldn't cooperate. She felt dizzy, uncoordinated, and confused. The more Richardson or Commander Eckert yelled, the more confused she got. The more confused she got, the more they yelled.

"Right, march," Commander Eckert shouted. A move she'd done hundreds of times, yet Paige couldn't make herself do it. She bumped into Erin, almost knocking her over. She heard Eckert shouting, but it was her mom's ramblings that filled her ears and her mind. "Collins!"

Erin froze in place. Paige stopped, staring at her uncoordinated feet. A pair of boots moved toward her. Paige didn't look up; she braced for the verbal blow. As rain landed on their shoulders and caps, soon the spit from Eckert's mouth also dotted Erin's uniform as he yelled at her.

Rain. Spit. Then tears welling up. Paige made herself look at Erin and willed Erin not to cry.

"What is wrong with you, cadet?" Eckert asked. Behind him, Richardson shouted more questions at Erin. Before she had time to answer, they'd cut her off with another question.

"If she doesn't have what it takes to be a solider," Eckert said, now speaking to the rest of the unit as if Erin wasn't there, "then maybe she should reconsider her options."

Faster and harder than the rain, the questions without answers from Eckert and Richardson continued. This wasn't about Erin, Paige knew; it was about discipline, order and obedience. Erin happened to be the wounded animal that walked into a trap.

"I should remind all of you," Eckert

bellowed, hands on hips, chest pushed out, "that the purpose of this unit is to develop citizens of character dedicated to serving their nation and community. And the way you develop character is by showing discipline, but Collins here—"

"That's enough," Paige said, her voice soft but sharp.

"What did you say, cadet?" Eckert asked.

Paige stared at the middle-aged man who suddenly seemed so very angry about something so small. This wasn't life or death, not even close. "I said, enough, leave Erin alone."

"If Collins can't take it," Eckert snapped, "she can hand in her uniform."

Erin said nothing, but standing next to her, Paige heard swallowed sobs. It was as if she could feel Erin's muscles tightening, pulse racing, and her heart breaking. Paige thought of the hurt and loss and sacrifice in her family, in Erin's, David's, Josie's, everyone's, and for what?

Maybe Blake was right; maybe none of this mattered. Paige's dad's body had come home in a wooden box; her mom lived her life out of a pillbox; and Paige felt boxed in by Eckert. Like the Texas sky above her, the world was gray, not black and white. Eckert started in on Erin again.

Paige stepped forward. "If you want her uniform, then you can have mine, too." She reached for her cap and handed it to Commander Eckert. She stared at the man's eyes, wild and almost out of control. A far cry from those of her mom, even if they were fruit of the same rotten military tree.

And then Paige never looked back as she walked, not marched, out of the parking lot.

14

"I'm going to David's house to study," Paige announced to her mom as she cleared the kitchen table of their two plates from the dinner Paige quickly had prepared.

"Where's Perry?" Paige's mom asked. Like most nights over the past few weeks, Perry hadn't joined them for dinner, nor would he be around for most of the evening. Paige knew he was in college, but she also knew Tracy and

Jacob had asked him to be around to support Paige and help out. Paige thought her brother maintained his state of denial about their mom's pill problem by avoiding the house after dark. The few times he was home, he'd stayed in his room, door closed, lights off, TV on.

"I don't know where he is."

"Oh."

"I'll be back from David's by midnight."

"Eleven, Pug."

"Midnight, Mom."

"Eleven."

"Fine, eleven thirty."

"I said eleven," Paige's mom said and sighed like she was in pain. "End of discussion."

Was it all adults or just those in the military, Paige thought, who assumed the world revolved around their ability to shout orders and the willingness of people like Paige to obey?

"If you're late, you're grounded for another week."

"I won't be late."

"If you are, then—"

Paige tossed the plate in her hand into the sink. It cracked in half. "And if I am late, you know what, you won't even notice, you'll be passed out or talking like a zombie on the phone."

"You clean that up and clean up your attitude. For a cadet, you don't have control—"

"I quit."

"You quit what?" her mom asked.

Paige said nothing.

"You quit ROTC?"

"Yes."

"Why would you do that, Pug?" Paige's mom's voice was a mix of hurt and anger.

"Why do you get to ask all the questions?"

"Because I'm your mother."

Paige took a deep breath. She'd told off her commander, and now she had strength to speak her mind at home. She had nothing to lose because all seemed lost. "You don't act like it."

Her mom twisted in her chair, wincing in pain. "Watch your step."

"You don't," Paige hissed. "You just stumble around this house at night like some drugged-out zombie, talking to your boyfriend on the phone, and popping pills like a junkie."

Paige's mom pushed herself out of her chair. "I said, watch your step."

Undeterred and more determined, Paige took a step toward her mother. "What are you going to do? Ground me? The minute your plane touched the ground, you brought me down. Perry and I were just fine living without you, not that you're here after sundown anyway."

Paige's mother took a step closer, but Paige didn't back down. Nose to nose, eye to eye.

"You don't know what you're talking about," her mom said. "You don't know the amount of pain I'm in on a daily basis. I'm crippled, useless, and unwanted."

"What happened? It wasn't like this last time you were—"

"I was stronger then; I had to be. You don't need to be strong sitting behind a desk."

"But you're safe and—"

"Maybe everyone would have been better off if I never came home, like your father. Is that it, Paige?"

Paige felt the beating of her heart so loud. It was a time bomb. And time was up.

"Yes."

"Leave, just leave me alone, Paige."

"That's easy." Then, turning her back, Paige said, "Because you taught me how."

15

"Paige, you shouldn't have done that," Erin said. "I could stand up for myself."

Paige started to disagree but let it go. Erin still wore the uniform; Paige didn't. It wasn't about Erin or Eckert, Paige knew. Like everything in the past month, it was about her mom.

"If you talk with Commander Eckert, I'm sure he'd let you back in," Josie added.

Paige continued her silence. So many

thoughts were running through her brain like a traffic jam after a Spurs game. David also remained silent. He'd told Paige he didn't agree with disobeying orders, and that he wouldn't quit as well, but he was proud of her for standing up for herself and Erin. Like most military kids, David respected strength and loyalty over all else.

"Paige, we're all in this together," Erin said.

"We can't do it without you," Josie said.

"Thanks, but I don't know, something just snapped," Paige said, unsure what to say. She'd yet to tell Erin and Josie about how bad her mom's problems were, wondering if they would understand. Would they feel sorry for her? And if so, would that make Paige feel ashamed? Paige wondered why her friends didn't ask why they were never invited to her house anymore.

"What did your mom say?" Alonzo asked. Josie rolled her eyes when he asked.

"She's not happy about it." Paige crossed her arms across her chest. "And I don't care."

"Cold," Alonzo whispered.

"You were so looking forward—" Josie began.

But Paige cut her off. "Look, I don't want to talk about it. About her."

David reached out his hand, but Paige kept her hands wrapped around herself. *The only person you can really trust, who can never let you down, is yourself,* she thought.

"You want to come over tonight?" David asked.

"I'm grounded again."

"That sucks."

"We'll text," Paige said and then faked a smile. When her mom was deployed, they kept in touch mainly by Skype or e-mail. Paige understood now that all the electrons flying in outer space only gave everyone the illusion they were still close and that the thousands of miles across the ocean didn't matter. Grounded, unable to see David during ROTC, Paige felt the closeness between them ready to slip through her fingers, like grains of sand in the Afghan desert.

Paige tried to rejoin the conversation, but Josie and Erin dominated, talking about the upcoming ROTC performance at the home football game and then the Veterans Day parade. As they spoke, Paige felt as if a thin wall had already formed; she was no longer one of them. All those bonds of the past, strained because they were not marching together.

"David, you'll still be my friend," Paige whispered.

David laughed, but Paige didn't even smile. She clutched onto his arm. "Always," he said, patting her hand.

No longer a cadet, Paige allowed herself the luxury of crying.

"What's wrong?" he asked.

Paige thought about all the lost parents, widowed partners, and broken children. People who thought they'd be together always and forever. "Always doesn't mean always anymore."

16

"Paige, don't you need to go to the football game?" Uncle Jacob asked.

Paige was torn. She wanted to see David, Josie, Erin, and her friends march before the game, but the thought of watching it from the stands hurt too much. It just made the wall between her and her former cadet comrades that much thicker.

"Paige, your uncle asked you—" Aunt Tracy started.

"I quit ROTC," Paige said. Like a tire going flat, her aunt and uncle gasped. The three sat outside on the porch like they'd done a hundred times, but Paige knew tonight was different.

"Whatever for?" Aunt Tracy asked.

She hadn't wanted to tell them. Paige wanted simply to come over for dinner, sit with her aunt and uncle, and talk about nothing much at all but make things normal, like they were before her mom came home. Yet, all the talk at the table had danced around her mom's return. If anyone knew Paige, it was her aunt and uncle who raised her more than her mother ever did.

"Commander Eckert was all over Erin," Paige started, but a voice in the back of her head shouted louder than the one coming from her mouth. *Tell the truth*, it said. *Tell the truth*.

"I'm sure your mother could arrange for you to—" Uncle Jacob started.

"I don't want her help," Paige said, almost spitting out each word. "With anything."

Her aunt and uncle looked at each other.

Paige knew the look: concern, worry. She'd seen it after her mother had deployed, before Perry's football games, and so many times when she'd failed and they'd consoled her. "Paige, what's going on?" Uncle Jacob asked.

"I can't."

"Paige, we're here for you; you know that," Aunt Tracy said.

"Really? Can I move back here?" Paige asked, words she never dreamed of saying.

"What's wrong?" her aunt asked again.

Paige put the glass of iced tea against her forehead, not so much to cool off but to slow down her racing thoughts. Where to start? What could she tell? What did they know?

"Mom."

"I know it must be hard having her back in the house," Uncle Jacob said. "But it takes time; you know that, you've been through this before. This time you're older, more independent, so . . ."

"That's part of it, but . . ."

"But."

Miles away, her friends were marching, the crowd was cheering, and the Sam Houston High Rockets were courageously facing down their opponents. Across the oceans, brave men and women of the US Military put their lives on the line. *Heroes*, Paige thought. *I'm a coward.*

Aunt Tracy left her deck chair, walked over to Paige, and knelt down next to her. She pushed her hair out of her face, kissed her on the cheek, and whispered, "What's wrong?"

"She's an addict," Paige confessed. "Oxy-Contin. Valium. She's a zombie most nights."

Her aunt winced as if she was in pain. "We know, Paige. We've tried to talk with her, but she won't even discuss it. I don't want to put you through more than you can handle, but your mom would be devastated if you moved out."

"If she's in so much pain, why doesn't she just retire and deal with it?" Paige asked.

"Her service is her life," Uncle Jacob said. "And nobody wants to be a veteran now."

Paige recalled horror stories from kids at

school about their vet parents waiting years to get help. But her mom needed help. She was strong, but like that plate in the sink, she was broken in half. Half of the day able to function, half a zombie. Half at home, half still deployed.

"We need to do something," Paige said. "An intervention like on TV."

"I don't think that would work with my sister," Uncle Jacob said. "Give her time, Paige."

"Why doesn't she get help from the Air Force?"

"I think she's afraid of letting them know. They have zero tolerance and it could affect her career. Don't worry. Your mom is a fighter. She'll kick it."

"And if she doesn't?" Paige asked. Her uncle answered with roaring silence.

17

"Tell me all about the game," Paige whispered into David's left ear. His right ear held an earbud from Paige's phone as they shared music.

They sat on the sofa in David's basement. David's Aunt Lita had long since gone to bed. "I'm glad you came over," David said. "I thought you were grounded."

"I am." She'd waited until her mother passed out before sneaking out of the house.

"Won't you get in trouble?"

Paige pushed herself closer to David. She could feel his ribs under his uniform that he still proudly wore. The knit of the uniform was tough, fibers held closely together.

"There's not much she can do," Paige said. She'd never been grounded by her aunt and uncle, never been in trouble at home or in school; this was all new to her, scary, exciting.

"What if she tells you that you can't see me again?" David asked.

Paige turned her head, kissed David like it was the last time, and said, "I'd kill myself."

"Paige, don't say things like that," David whispered.

Paige paused. She'd heard stories at school about students trying to kill themselves. There were so many stories that at least one had to be true. If her mom took David away, Paige thought, she'd have nothing left to live for. Why live a life of pain and loss?

"Promise me," David said in his most serious

voice. "Promise me you won't . . ."

Paige kissed him again. "David, I promise I won't kill myself."

David pulled Paige tighter. She wrapped David around her like a warm blanket on a rare, cold San Antonio night and let the music fill their ears since there was nothing left to say.

* * *

David was asleep when Paige woke up. It was four in the morning. Paige picked up her purse and snuck up the stairs and out the door. She rode her bike toward home, helmet off, letting the sounds of early morning San Antonio, including the roar of Air Force planes, fill her ears.

Perry's truck was in the driveway. Paige figured like most nights, he'd arrived home a little after 2 a.m., closing time at the local bars. She saw him rarely, like he was getting her ready for next summer and the rest of her life when he'd be more memory than man.

The house was dark, save for a hall light.

Silent, save for the hum of the air conditioner, and something else, from the living room. Like water going down after clearing a clogged drain.

Her mom, on the sofa, on her back. Her phone cradled on her chest, the dim light from it illuminating her face. No makeup. Her short hair unwashed, messy. Her cheeks wet.

"You'll be home soon," Paige's mom mumbled, or something like it. She'd say something, go silent, try but fail to speak again. Paige thought this wasn't how a mom was supposed to look. She looked more like a baby trying to learn to walk, talk, become a person. Her mom wasn't a person, at least not after dark. "I love you, Captain."

Paige ripped the phone from her mom's hand and put it against her ear. There was a man's voice. "Who is this?" Paige shouted, but the voice kept talking over her, like he couldn't even hear her. Frustrated, Paige ended the call. Last dialed: voicemail. "Mom, wake up!"

Paige's mother mumbled. She tried to sit up but couldn't. "What?"

"Mom, who are you talking to?" Paige shouted. Her mom's eyes rolled back in her head. Paige grabbed her mom by the shoulders, lifted her up, and screamed, "Wake up!"

Her mom's heavy eyelids opened slowly but closed quickly. Paige pushed her mother back on the sofa and stared up at the ceiling. "Is that you, Pug?" her mom mumbled.

Paige knelt by the sofa, rested her head on her mom's chest. "It's me, Mom," said Paige. Except she wasn't Pug anymore, and her mom was Mom only in name, not in action.

18

OCTOBER 31 / HALLOWEEN NIGHT
HARKINS' HOUSE

"Trick or treat!" Paige heard kids yell from outside the front door, far from where she stood. Her mom sat in a chair by the front door handing out candy. She had been unable to convince Paige to join her, do it herself, or go trick-or-treating ("You used to love that").

While her mom handed out candy, Paige gathered up pills from her mom's room. Paige filled the bag with OxyContin but also with other pills, like Valium, muscle relaxers, antidepressants, and sleeping pills. It was a pharmacy of addiction.

Once she gathered up the pills, Paige told her mother she was going to study. She shut her bedroom door, put in her earbuds, opened up her chemistry book, and waited. Like a unit arranging an ambush, Paige just needed patience to get the enemy out into the light of day.

The doorbell stopped ringing after eight and Paige heard her mom's end-of-day ritual. She was slowly checking that all the windows were closed and locked, opening the refrigerator, opening the Lone Star Light, closing the fridge door. Then she walked slowly toward the bathroom. No pills there. Her mom rarely had them out in the open. A secret. A secret about to be revealed.

The bathroom door opened. "Good night, Pug," her mom whispered outside Paige's door. Her mom's bedroom door opened and closed. Paige rose from her bed, left her room, and knelt by her mom's door. She wanted to hear it all. The drawer opened, closed, and opened again as if the results would be different. The second time, the drawer wasn't shut, it was slammed. Then the next drawer and the next. Like mortar fire with seconds between blasts, the drawers exploded with angry slams.

Then silence. Absolute silence, as though her mom had stopped breathing. Paige stared at the wedding photo of her parents on the hall wall. Her dad in uniform, her mom pregnant, their lives full of hope, all dead in Afghanistan. How?

She had her mom's pills, her quid; Paige needed the quo. She needed to know. She tiptoed back to her room to wait.

The knock at the door was louder than she imagined. Like thunder. "Paige!"

Paige locked the door just as her mom pulled on the knob. "Paige, open up!"

More knocking that turned to pounding and finally kicking. Neither the door nor Paige would budge. Paige heard her mom's heavy breathing, the cursing, and the sounds of pain.

"Paige, I don't know what you're thinking, but you open this door now."

"How did he die?" Paige shouted. "Tell me and I'll open the door." Paige made no promises about giving her back her pills. Fighting one fire at a time.

Silence. Then Paige heard her mother slide to the floor. On her side of the door, Paige did the same. A light sound, maybe her mom's palm pressed on the door, followed. Paige put her hand against the door. Where once oceans separated them, now just one wooden door. One truth.

"I never told you, Paige, because you didn't need to know the horror of war," her mom said slowly. "He was traveling in a convoy away from the base. They came upon a group of boys playing. One was a little older than Perry, about nine. He asked your father for water."

Paige closed her eyes and tried to imagine

the scene of a nine-year-old Iraqi boy.

"Your father handed the kid his canteen," Paige's mom said, her voice shaking. "When he handed it back, the boy took out a knife and stabbed your father in the side. Just then, a man came out with an AK and opened fire. The squad handled the man; your father shot the boy."

Paige looked at a photo of her dad on her desk. He'd never seemed so alive to her than in this long-overdue story of his death. "They couldn't stitch him up?   He didn't bleed to death, did he?"

"He never got the image of shooting that young boy out of his head," Paige's mom whispered. "No matter what he did, where he went, he kept thinking of that boy's face."

"It was war," Paige said. "He didn't have any choice but to shoot him, no matter—"

"That's what I told him, but he didn't listen," her mom said. "He came back home. You were little. You don't remember, but then he got deployed again. For the last time."

"Mom, I don't understand, didn't he die when that boy—"

"He died that day, Paige, his soul did at least, but his body kept living, fulfilling his mission, until it all just got to be too much for him. Paige, your father killed himself."

Paige's mouth opened, but no words came. Instead, a yelp, like a dog hit by a car.

"Every soldier deals with the pain of war in a different way," her mom said. "Your father couldn't handle his pain, but I'm trying to manage mine the best I can. Open the door."

"Mom, you're killing yourself, too."

"Open the door, Paige."

"Mom, you've got to stop."

"You don't think I know that?" A fist pounded against the door. Paige reached into the bag and pulled out a bottle of OxyContin. After opening the bottle, she balanced one pill on her fingertip and slipped it under the door like a peace offering. "Open the door, Paige."

"No."

Her mom pounded the door again, but then Paige heard her stand and walk away toward the kitchen. Was she coming back with a knife? A few second later, Paige heard her mother sit down outside the door. Silence and then her mom's voice: "Hello, is this Lita Garcia?"

Paige clawed at the door. "Don't you dare!"

"Mrs. Garcia, this is Helen Harkins, Paige's mother," her mom said, each word slicing Paige as deeply as the knife had sliced her dad's skin. "We need to talk about your son and—"

Paige unlocked the door and hurled the bag of pills at her mother. "I wish you'd never come home."

Her mother grabbed the bag, told Mrs. Garcia she had to go, and retreated toward her room, but didn't disagree.

19

"I'm so sorry, Commander Eckert," Paige said, pleading her case.

"Rank insubordination," he answered. Eckert, also a history teacher at the school, sat behind his desk. Paige stood in front of him, feeling naked and lost without her uniform.

"Why do you deserve a second chance in my unit?" Eckert asked.

Paige stood as straight and tall as any cadet

had ever stood in front of Eckert. "Because both of my parents served. One died, one came back wounded. Because we all make mistakes and mine was protecting another cadet. Mine was a mistake of pride and loyalty, not weakness."

Eckert scratched his bald head and fumbled with papers on his desk.

"Sir, I will do anything you ask, anything you say. This matters more to me than anything." Paige lied to him. David mattered most. She had traded her mom's bag of pills to make sure she'd stay with David. She vowed to herself never to be put in that position again. If her mother would go to those extremes, then Paige knew she'd have to go one more. It was war.

"I had a very convincing call from your mother this morning," Eckert said.

Paige stayed still, her fists clenched. She didn't want her mother's help. *If my mother is going to help anyone,* Paige thought, *she should start with herself.* "Sir, I didn't ask—"

"She told me that," Eckert said. "I wasn't

going to tell you, but I thought you should know that she's concerned about you. We both agreed that what you need most right now is discipline, not to be disciplined. I'll see you at six on Friday morning. Dismissed!"

Paige saluted Commander Eckert and marched military style to the door. Once outside, she reached for her phone. David? Josie? Erin? No, someone else. Like everything else about her mom, Paige's emotions slammed against each other. She was happy to be back in the unit, but she didn't need her mom to fix things.

"You've reached Capt. Helen Harkins. I'm not—" Paige stopped the call.

Of course, she thought, the voice on her mom's phone. The voicemail she listened to. It had to be. Her dad.

20

"We missed you, Paige." Josie hugged Paige as their ROTC unit disbanded at Milam Park. Erin, David, and Alonzo huddled next to Paige, sharing the same sentiments.

"I'm so happy to be back," Paige said. "It was only a little while without you guys, this unit, but it felt so much longer. Being in this unit made me feel part of something. Thank you."

"Why do I feel like you're making some

kind of farewell speech?" Alonzo said.

"You are part of something," David whispered and reached out for her. "Us."

But Paige backed away. "Hey, David, no PDA in uniform. I can't risk anything."

"Well, maybe later out of uniform," David said.

Paige laughed. "How much out of uniform?" she asked, embarrassed, but also intrigued.

David laughed. "What was with that phone call from your mom? My aunt thought it was so odd. I mean, they haven't met and out of the blue, your mom calls but then hangs up on her?"

"David, follow me." Paige pulled on David's arm, leading him away from the unit.

"What's going on?" David asked. Paige sat down on a park bench; David sat next to her.

"I'm going to tell you some things you need to know," Paige said softly. In the distance, she could still hear bands playing and crowds cheering. Her unit had led the parade, but the mile-long route was still filled with school bands, ROTC units, veterans' group, and active duty units, including her mother's. Somewhere her mom sat in an Air Force vehicle being cheered. It made what she was about to say, and then do, feel even stranger than she could have imagined.

"You can tell me anything, Paige. I won't tell a soul. Promise."

Paige studied the dirt below her boots on the ground. "Some promises are hard to keep."

"I'll never break a promise to you," David whispered.

Paige knew what she was supposed to say in return but couldn't form the words. "David, my mom came home with a problem. She's hooked on pain pills. It's so hard."

"Never mind the PDA rules." David pulled Paige toward him and held her tight. With his arms steadying her, Paige told David about her mom and her own inability to do anything about it.

"She needs to get into treatment," David said. "There's no shame to it."

"I know it and she knows it, but she can't face it. There's only one thing to do."

"What's that?"

"Drastic times call for drastic measures. I hope you understand and you know how much I love you." Paige kissed David, defeating his attempts to question her.

Rules, like promises, Paige thought, were easily made in good times, and just as easily broken in desperate days.

* * *

Paige kicked down her mother's door and used a crowbar to pry open the new locked desk where, no doubt, her mom stored her pills. The first cache was small, but it was enough. Paige examined the bottles. A different doctor for each prescription. Dr. Thompson had prescribed the Valium that Paige buried in the pocket of her perfectly pressed ROTC pants. Paige checked her phone again. Her mother had said she'd be home for dinner at six. It was five.

Paige went into the kitchen, opened the fridge, and grabbed a can of Lone Star. Like she'd heard her mother do every night, she popped open the can, and took a nasty sip. She opened the nearly full bottle of pills and dumped all but two in the sink, grinding them up in the garbage disposal. Putting the pill bottle in her pocket and tucking the beer under her arm, Paige stopped at the kitchen counter and picked up a single sheet of paper and a black marker, and she grabbed a stapler from the drawer.

Paige opened the bottle, swallowed two Valiums, and washed them down with the rest of the Lone Star. Slowly she walked to the sofa that she'd seen her mom pass out on so many times. *That crap*, Paige thought, *ends today.*

On the single sheet of paper, she wrote the words and then stapled the paper to her uniform, right in the middle over her heart. As she shut her eyes, she imagined her mom walking in the door and seeing Paige lying there and then reading the note.

Mom, this is what it is like to live with you. Tell David I'm sorry I broke my promise. I love you. Get help. Goodbye.

20

"Paige, can you hear me?"

Paige slowly opened her eyes and just as slowly took in her surroundings: she was in a hospital room. She tried to raise her arm to wipe her eyes clear, but they were restrained.

"It's just a precaution," Paige's mom whispered. Her aunt and uncle stood behind Paige's mom, whose wooden chair scraped against the metal hospital bed. Perry stood in the corner, arms crossed, head down like it weighed a hundred pounds.

"I'm sorry, Mom."

"You should be!" Perry shouted from across the room. "What a stupid stunt. How—"

"Perry, please, now isn't the time!" Paige's mom said. Perry cursed loudly at his sister and then stormed out of the room. "Paige, I don't understand what you were thinking."

Paige remembered writing the note and swallowing the pills but nothing after. Had Perry found her? Her mother? Did David know? But most of all, Paige wondered, did it matter?

"Mom, you do know why I did it, don't you?" Paige said. Her mouth felt dry.

Paige's mom nodded over and over, like someone praying. "I know."

"What are you going to do?" Paige asked.

No nods, no tears, no words, just the clicks and beeps of machines.

"Mom, please."

Paige could see her aunt and uncle closing in.

Each of them put a hand on her mom's shoulder like guardian angels.

"You told me after I landed that you called that my freedom flight," Paige's mom said slowly, "But I'm not free, am I?"

Paige swallowed her words just as her mother, Paige thought, had to swallow her pride.

"I fought for freedom for others," her mom said. "I need to fight now for my own."

22

"Mom, stop using so many acronyms," Paige said into the phone as her mom rambled on about the ADAPT rehab program at the Travis Air Force Base medical center in California. Her aunt and uncle stood beside her, but Perry sat in the other room watching football.

"I'm sorry, Pug," her mom said. "And I'm sorry I missed Thanksgiving dinner."

"We'll save you a plate," Aunt Tracy said.

"Will you be home for Christmas?" Paige asked.

In the other room, the football crowd roared, but the phone brought nothing but silence.

"Mom?"

"I don't know, it depends on my progress," her mom started and then explained the ADAPT program, ending with nothing but praise for her treatment team.

"That all sounds promising, Helen," Uncle Jacob said.

"Is Perry there?" Paige's mom asked. Paige looked at her aunt and uncle, hoping that one of them would answer. When her mom was overseas, they spoke on Skype. For once, she was glad her mom couldn't see her. "It's a simple question. I know he's angry at me."

"And me." Since he'd stormed out of the hospital room, Perry had refused to speak to Paige. He spent more nights at friend's houses, doing everything to avoid his sister. Even at Thanksgiving dinner, he'd said nothing more than necessary and left the table while still chewing his last bite.

Paige's mom sighed deeply. "I know he thinks this will ruin my career, and maybe—"

"But it will save your life. Isn't that more important?"

"When you're in the Air Force, they're one and the same. Perry knows that."

Paige thought about her friends, thought about David; they didn't associate the military with life but with death. She hadn't told David what she did and felt wrong keeping it a secret, but figured maybe like her mom never telling her about her dad's death, some secrets should stay hidden.

"Look, I'll fight this and I'll beat it," her mom said forcefully. "I was strong when I was in country, but I let myself get weak when I came home. I thought I could handle it. I was wrong. I'm not leaving my children orphans; I'm not giving the war another casualty."

Paige knew just saying "I was wrong" was a big step for her mom.

"I'm not the only one." Paige's mom rattled off statistics about vets and active duty personnel like herself with painkiller addiction. "We've got each other and our treatment team."

Paige thought about all the teams and groups she'd depended on to help her through hard times, but she knew it was her family that mattered most, even if Perry had turned his back on her.

"Listen, Paige, what you did was dangerous, you could have—"

"I was desperate, Mom," Paige said. "I made it look worse than it was, but it worked."

The phone went silent. "Mom, are you okay?"

"Not yet, Pug, but I will be the next time you see me."

Paige started to speak, but stopped when she heard an odd sound on the other end of the phone: crying. It was everything Paige needed to know. It doesn't matter whether cadets or soldiers cry. They live. They die. They fight.

ABOUT THE AUTHOR

Patrick Jones is the author of more than twenty novels for teens. He has also written two nonfiction books about combat sports, *The Main Event*, on professional wrestling, and *Ultimate Fighting*, on mixed martial arts. He has spoken to students at more than one hundred alternative schools, including residents of juvenile correctional facilities. Find him on the web at www.connectingya.com and on Twitter: @PatrickJonesYA.

2 1982 02880

ALWAYS
FAITHFUL
PATRICK JONES

COLLATERAL
DAMAGE
PATRICK JONES / BRENT CHARTIER

COMBAT
ZONE
PATRICK JONES

FREEDOM
FLIGHT
PATRICK JONES

CHECK OUT ALL OF THE TITLES IN T
SUPPORT AND DEFEND SERIES